The Never Girls

into
the
waves

Written by
Kiki Thorpe

Illustrated by
Jana Christy

A STEPPING STONE BOOK™

RANDOM HOUSE 🏠 NEW YORK

For Lila
—*K.T.*

For my favorite mermaid, Sophia Elizabeth Jackson
—*J.C.*

Library of Congress Cataloging-in-Publication Data is available upon request.

ISBN 978-0-7364-3525-3 (paperback) — ISBN 978-0-7364-8205-9 (lib.bdg.) —
ISBN 978-0-7364-3526-0 (ebook)

randomhousekids.com/disney
Printed in the United States of America
10 9 8 7 6 5 4 3 2 1

This book has been officially leveled by using the F&P Text Level Gradient™ Leveling System.

Never Land

Far away from the world we know, on the distant seas of dreams, lies an island called Never Land. It is a place full of magic, where mermaids sing, fairies play, and children never grow up. Adventures happen every day, and anything is possible.

There are two ways to reach Never Land. One is to find the island yourself. The other is for it to find you. Finding Never Land on your own takes a lot of luck and a pinch of fairy dust. Even then, you will only find the island if it wants to be found.

Every once in a while, Never Land drifts close to our world . . . so close a fairy's laugh slips through. And every once in an even longer while, Never Land opens its doors to a special few. Believing in magic and fairies from the bottom of your heart can make the extraordinary happen. If you suddenly hear tiny bells or feel a sea breeze where there is no sea, pay careful attention. Never Land may be close by. You could find yourself there in the blink of an eye.

One day, four special girls came to Never Land in just this way. This is their story.

Never Land

Pirate Cove

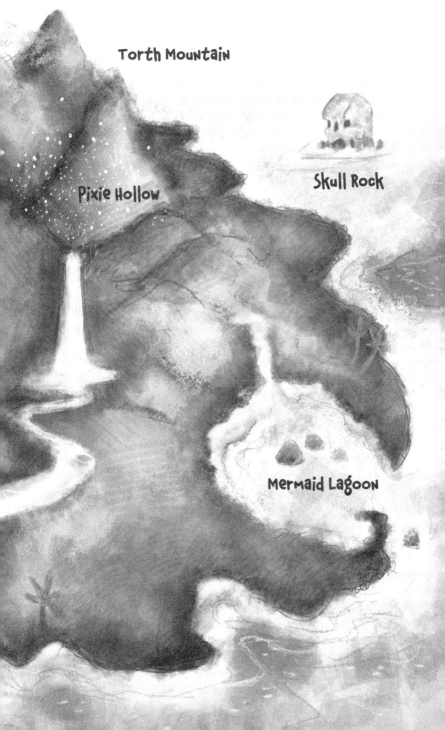

Chapter 1

"How about this one?" Kate McCrady asked. She poked her finger at the glass wall of a fish tank. Behind it, a blue-and-gold-striped fish darted by.

Lainey Winters studied the fish carefully. "He looks kind of grumpy, don't you think?"

"What about this one?" On Lainey's other side, Mia Vasquez pointed to an inky black fish with fins as flowy as silk scarves.

Lainey shook her head. "Too fancy."

Kate sighed. "I think we've looked at every single fish in the pet store. Just pick one, Lainey."

"I'm *trying,*" Lainey said. It was a big decision! She was finally getting a pet—her first pet ever. She had to make sure she chose the right one.

Lainey had wanted a pet for as long as she could remember. But her parents didn't love animals as much as she did. For months Lainey had done all her chores and saved her allowance, and at last they'd given in.

"Maybe we should look at some other animals," Mia suggested.

"You mean like that one?" Kate pointed to the tank behind her.

Mia turned and sprang back with a

squeal. A spiky brown lizard was staring at her from behind the glass.

Kate laughed. "What's the matter? He won't hurt you."

Mia shuddered. "Lizards give me the creeps."

"Well, I can't get one anyway," Lainey said. "My mom and dad don't want anything that could get lost in the house. That includes lizards."

"Thank goodness," Mia said.

"How about a bird, then?" Kate asked.

"I don't like birds in cages," Lainey said.

"It's too bad you can't get a dog or a cat," Mia said.

"I know. But my parents are allergic," Lainey said. "No, I've decided on a fish. I just have to find the right one."

Lainey walked past the fish tanks again. There were so many fish to choose from! Big ones, little ones. Some were bright as jewels, while others were so drab they looked like rocks. But where was *her* fish?

Lainey stopped to watch dozens of bright orange fish swimming back and forth. The sign on the tank read GOLDFISH: MEDIUM.

As she stood there, one fish swam right up to the glass. "Hi, little fella," Lainey said.

The goldfish waved his fins. He seemed to be saying hello.

"Hey," Lainey said. "I think he likes me!"

Mia and Kate came over to see. "He's really cute," Mia said.

"Look at his top fin!" Kate said.

The fin on the little fish's back seemed to stick up more than the other goldfishes' fins.

The fish swam away, then came back to look at Lainey. She grinned. "Guys, I think I found my fish!"

"Finally!" Kate said.

Lainey waited while Mia went to

find the saleswoman, who was chatting with Lainey's mom. They watched as she scooped the little fish out with a net. She handed the fish to Lainey in a plastic bag filled with water.

With the money she'd saved, Lainey bought a fishbowl, fish food, some rocks, and a little plastic castle for her fish to play in. She listened carefully as the saleswoman explained how to feed the fish and how to clean his bowl. Kate and Mia helped her carry everything out to the car.

"What are you going to name him?" Lainey's mother asked as they drove home.

"How about Shimmer, since he's so shiny?" Mia suggested.

"Or Finley," Kate said. "Get it? *Fin*-ley?"

Lainey looked at her fish swimming

in his bag. He looked like a bright spot of sunlight. "I'm going to call him Sunshine," she decided. "Sunshine Shimmer Finley Goldfish."

Her mom laughed. "That's a big name for a little fish."

"Then I'll call him Sunny for short." Lainey held him up close to her face. "Do you like your name, Sunny?"

Sunny opened and closed his mouth. Lainey couldn't be sure, but it looked as if he was saying yes.

✳

Back at Lainey's house, Kate and Mia helped Lainey set up Sunny's fishbowl. They put in the rocks and the castle, then filled the bowl with water. When Sunny was settled in his new home, Lainey dropped a pinch of fish food inside. They watched him gobble up the flakes.

"I think he likes it here," Mia said.

He does seem happy. But how can I be sure? Lainey wondered. Did Sunny really like his new home? What did he like to do? With a dog you could throw a ball or a stick. But how did you play with a goldfish?

Lainey realized she didn't know anything about what made a goldfish happy. But she knew someone who did. She picked up Sunny's bowl. "Come on," she said to her friends. "We've got to go to Pixie Hollow."

Mia and Kate looked surprised.

"With Sunny?" Mia asked.

"Yes. I want him to meet Fawn," Lainey said. Fawn was an animal-talent fairy. She could talk to any creature, feathered, finned, or furred. She'd be able to find out what Sunny was really thinking.

"At least let me help you carry the bowl," said Kate.

Together, Lainey and Kate carried the fishbowl out of her room and down the stairs. It was harder than Lainey had thought. The fishbowl was heavy and difficult to grasp. They had to be extra careful not to spill a drop.

On the bottom step, they stopped to rest. "Maybe we should just *tell* the fairies about Sunny," Kate said.

Lainey pushed up her glasses, which

were slipping down her nose. "No, I want Sunny to see Pixie Hollow for himself." Turning to Sunny, she said, "You're going to love it, little fella." Then she unscrewed the cap of the fish food and gave him another pinch.

"Are you sure you should give him more food?" Mia asked. "The woman at the pet store said to feed him only twice a day."

"But he's hungry. See?" Lainey pointed. Sunny was devouring the food as if he hadn't eaten in weeks.

When Sunny had finished eating, Lainey picked up the bowl again. "Let's go."

The way to Pixie Hollow lay behind a loose fence board in Mia's backyard, two houses down from Lainey's. The girls had discovered the magical portal the summer before. Since then, the portal had moved three times, and each time Lainey and her friends had had to find it again. But no matter how many times it moved, it always led them back to the fairies.

As they reached Mia's house, Lainey hoped the portal hadn't moved again. She wasn't sure how much farther she could carry Sunny's bowl.

Mia's little sister, Gabby, was playing in the backyard. Though there were still patches of snow on the ground, she was holding a watering can. Gabby hummed to herself as she watered some invisible flowers. When she saw the fishbowl, though, she came running over. "What's that?"

"It's Lainey's new pet. Be *careful,* Gabby,"

Mia said as her sister jostled in for a closer look.

"Neato!" Gabby leaned in so far, her nose almost stuck to the bowl. "You should name him Spike."

"He already has a name," Lainey said. "It's Sunny, and we're taking him to meet the fairies."

"Yay!" Gabby ran to the loose fence board, the fairy wings she always wore bouncing behind her.

Lainey held her breath as Gabby pushed on the board. Through the gap in the fence, she could see a sliver of sky bluer than anything in this world. Lainey's breath whooshed out. Never Land was right where they'd left it.

Lainey and Kate carried the fishbowl

to the hole, passing it between them as they wriggled through. They came out in a forest on the other side. Golden sunlight spilled down between the trees, and the ground was springy with moss.

"There it is, Sunny. Isn't it beautiful?" Lainey cried. Ahead stood the giant Home Tree, where the fairies lived. Its branches were dotted with windows and doors. Even after so many visits, it still took Lainey's breath away.

All that was left was to cross Havendish Stream. Holding Sunny in her arms, Lainey started across the stepping-stones.

"Oh no!" Lainey's foot slipped. The fishbowl tipped. "Sunny!"

"Gotcha!" Kate grabbed Lainey before she could fall. Water sloshed out of the

bowl. But Sunny was safe inside.

On the far bank, Lainey set down Sunny's bowl with shaking arms. "Thanks, Kate. That was close."

"Maybe you should leave Sunny here while we find Fawn," Kate said. "You can't carry that bowl all over Pixie Hollow."

"I guess you're right," Lainey said. But she didn't want to leave Sunny sitting there. She looked around for a safe place to put him.

Just downstream, a hollow in the bank formed a shallow, still pool of water. Lainey placed Sunny's bowl in the water, adding a few rocks around it to hold it in place.

There. That was good. *Maybe Sunny will even like seeing some of Pixie Hollow underwater,* Lainey thought.

"I'll be back soon," she told him. "You'll be okay. Right, little fella?"

Sunny opened and closed his mouth. Lainey took that as a yes. She gave him a wave. Then she headed off with her friends to find Fawn.

Chapter 2

Rani stood on the bank of Havendish Stream, letting her bare toes squish in the mud. She watched the water flowing past, reading its surface like a map. Here, near the bank, the water was still and calm. But out beyond the rocks, she could see swirling eddies and the ripples of the current. *It's moving fast today,* she thought. *I'll have to keep close to shore.*

Rani was a water-talent fairy. She could hold a raindrop in her hands and shape

it like clay, or coax a rivulet from a pond like a snake charmer. She could make water do her bidding—but she was never foolish enough to think that she was more powerful.

She dove into the stream, feeling a burst of joy as the water closed in around her. Rani was happiest when she was swimming. Most Never fairies couldn't swim—their wings became waterlogged and pulled them down. But Rani didn't have any wings—she'd lost them many years ago. And even though she missed them, she found that gliding through the water was a lot like flying. Sometimes it was even better.

Rani kicked her legs, pretending she was a mermaid. Her long blond hair waved behind her like seaweed. She turned over on her back and looked up through the water. The sky waved and shimmered, as if she were looking up at a lake.

This was her favorite place to swim. A bend in the stream made a natural swimming hole. Rani was careful never to swim too far out, where the current could sweep her away like a leaf.

Rani surfaced and took a breath, then dove again. She put her arms down at her sides and kicked her make-believe mermaid tail, gliding forward to—

Slam! Rani crashed headfirst into an invisible wall.

"Ouch!" She came up clutching her head. Already she could feel a bump forming.

"What in the name of Never Land?!"

There was a glass wall in the water! It reached from the bottom of the stream to well above the surface. But where had it come from?

Rani tried to swim around it and discovered that it curved. She paddled along, following it, until she was right back where she'd started. *It's like a bowl,* she thought. *A great big glass bowl.*

Just then, Rani spotted movement on the other side of the wall. Something gold darted past. There was a fish inside the bowl! Rani watched it swim back and forth. It seemed to be looking for a way out.

"It must have gotten trapped, poor little thing," she said to herself. She tapped on the glass. "Don't worry. I'm going to help you," she called.

Rani couldn't tell whether the fish understood. It stared at her, its mouth opening and closing silently. *He looks hungry,* she thought. *I wonder how long he's been in there.*

She swam all the way around the bowl again, feeling her way up and down the

glass, but she couldn't find an opening. The next time she went up for air, she noticed a hole at the top. *He must have jumped inside,* she thought.

Rani tried climbing up to the opening, but the glass was too slippery. She tried throwing a rock against the glass, but her little pebble bounced away without making a dent. The glass was thicker than it appeared.

Rani swam underwater again. Now she saw that the bowl's round bottom was wedged against a large stone. Perhaps if she could move it . . .

Rani pushed against the rock and felt it shift slightly. She swam up to the surface, took a breath, and dove down again.

It took Rani four tries, but at last the stone rolled out of the way. She swam aside as the heavy bowl tipped into the water.

Rani came up just in time to see the fish swim out through the opening. "Go, little fish! Be free!" she cried happily as the fish darted away.

Just then, she heard shouting from the bank. Rani turned to see the four Clumsy girls—Kate, Mia, Lainey, and Gabby—running toward her, with Fawn flying behind. One of the girls, Lainey, was waving her arms and shouting. It took Rani a moment to realize what she was saying.

"Help!" Lainey cried. "Stop him! My fish is getting away!"

Chapter 3

"Sunny, come back!" Lainey yelled, running alongside the stream. She could see her little fish flashing through the shallow water. If only he'd slow down!

At last, Sunny paused. Lainey plunged into the stream to grab him—

Splash! She fell face-first into the water. When she came up, her glasses were gone—and her hands were empty.

Lainey's friends came running up behind her. Kate and Mia helped her out of the water, while Gabby fished out her glasses and handed them back to Lainey.

"Are you okay?" Kate asked.

Lainey shook her head. "I lost Sunny," she said.

"Oh, Lainey." Mia put an arm around her.

"It's my fault," said Rani.

Lainey looked over. The water fairy stood dripping on a nearby rock. Rani always looked smaller than the other fairies because she had no wings. Now, soaked to the skin, she seemed even tinier.

"I thought he was trapped," Rani explained. "I just wanted to help. I didn't realize he was your pet. I'd fly backward if I could."

She looked so sorry. Lainey could tell
Rani wanted her to say something like "It's
okay." But it wasn't okay. Sunny was gone,
probably for good. The thought made
Lainey's eyes fill with tears.

"Don't cry, Lainey. We'll find him,"
Fawn said, fluttering over.

Lainey sniffled. "How?"

"We'll follow the stream and find out

where he went. I'll talk to every minnow I see if I have to," Fawn said.

"I can come, too," Rani said, brightening. "I'll look for him underwater."

"You will?" asked Lainey.

"Of course," the water fairy said. "It's the least I can do."

Lainey wiped her eyes, feeling a pinprick of hope. If Fawn and Rani thought they could find Sunny, maybe they really could. "But he was going so fast. How will we ever catch up with him?"

Fawn thought for a moment. "We'll need a boat," she said.

They all looked to the tree-root dock where the fairy boats were tied. There were rafts made from twigs, canoes made from seedpods, and tiny sloops with maple-leaf sails. But of course, none of them were big enough to hold four human girls.

"A boat, " Mia murmured, her eyes suddenly widening. "Hey! I think I have an idea."

✳

Moments later, the girls were back at Mia and Gabby's house. Lainey changed into some dry clothes she borrowed from Mia, then followed her friends down to the storage room in the basement.

"What are we looking for?" asked Kate as they poked among the boxes and old furniture.

"Our boat!" said Mia.

"We have a boat?" Gabby asked.

"Don't you remember? Papi bought a raft that time we rented a cabin by the lake," Mia said.

"Oh yeah!" Gabby said. "Papi took us for a boat ride, and you started screaming because you thought you saw an alligator. But it was just a stick."

Kate laughed. "You were scared of a stick?"

"It was a *big* stick," Mia said.

Gabby laughed, too. "You were yelling and waving your arms. You almost tipped the boat over. It was really funny."

Mia frowned at her sister. "Gabby, why don't you go and pack some sandwiches, or something."

"Okay." Gabby sighed and went upstairs.

Mia found the deflated raft rolled up behind a stack of boxes. She pulled it out and dusted it off.

"How do we blow it up?" asked Kate.

"There's a pump somewhere," said Mia.

After another search, she found the pump next to a pair of plastic paddles and two life jackets. "Gabby should wear  a life jacket since she's the littlest," she decided. "Lainey, you can wear the other." Lainey's friends knew she wasn't the strongest swimmer.

"Great. Can we go now?" Lainey said. For every minute they spent at home, hours could pass in Never Land. She was worried that by the time they got back, Sunny would be long gone.

Upstairs, they found Gabby in the kitchen. "I got the food!" she said, holding up her backpack.

"Good job," Kate said. "Come on."

"Leave your wings here, Gabby," Mia said. "You won't be able to wear them with the life jacket and backpack."

The girls headed for the yard. But as they were dragging the raft across the lawn, they heard a knock on the kitchen window.

"Uh-oh. It's Mami," Mia said.

Mrs. Vasquez opened the back door. "What on earth are you girls planning to do with that old raft?" she asked.

The friends glanced at one another. "Um . . . ," Mia said.

"Well . . . ," said Kate.

"Er . . . ," said Lainey.

"We're taking it to Never Land, Mami," Gabby piped up. "Lainey lost her goldfish, and we're going to float down Havendish Stream with the fairies and talk to some animals to see if we can find him."

Mrs. Vasquez blinked. Then she smiled. "All right, girls. Have fun. Just remember to put everything away when you're done." She went back into the house, closing the door behind her.

"I can't believe that worked," Kate said.

Gabby shrugged. "Sometimes it's better just to tell the truth." She pushed the loose fence board aside. "Come on. Let's go find Sunny!"

Chapter 4

A short time later, Lainey and her friends stood on the bank of Havendish Stream. They stared down at the yellow plastic raft bobbing gently on the water.

"When you said 'boat,' I pictured something bigger," Lainey said to Mia.

"Well, it *seemed* big last summer," Mia replied. "But I guess I was smaller then."

Inflated, the raft looked barely large enough to hold them all. *It's just a pool float,*

Lainey thought, eyeing the built-in cup holder. It didn't seem sturdy enough to go down a river. But it would have to do. Lainey knew they couldn't waste another minute. Poor Sunny was out there somewhere, and he needed her help.

The girls all climbed in. It really was a tight squeeze. But at last they managed to fit, with Lainey sitting in front as lookout, Kate and Mia paddling, and Gabby in the middle. Rani rode in the cup holder, which turned out to be the perfect size for a fairy. Fawn rode up front with Lainey.

They were about to push off, when Lainey suddenly cried, "Wait!"

She climbed out of the raft and ran up the bank to where she'd left Sunny's fishbowl. "I'll need this to bring him home," she explained as she carried it to the raft.

"Good thinking, Lainey," Mia said.

Cradling the bowl in her arms, Lainey climbed back in. Mia and Kate dug in their paddles and they floated out into the current.

They drifted past the Home Tree. Laundry-talent fairies were outside, hanging up the wash. Rows of bright petal dresses fluttered in the breeze like flags. Farther downstream, they passed tiny wooden doors set into the mossy bank— the workshops of the boat-making fairies. The stream wound through the orchard, and they saw the harvest-talent fairies up in the trees, working three to a plum.

It was different, seeing Pixie Hollow from a boat. Lainey would have enjoyed

it more if she weren't so worried about
Sunny. *Where is he?* she wondered. *What's he
doing? Is he okay?*

A dragonfly flew past. Fawn called to
it by buzzing her wings. *Bzzzzzz. Bzzzzzz.
Bzzzzzz.* The dragonfly flew in a circle
around them. Fawn listened, then nodded.

"He hasn't seen any fish that look like

Sunny," she reported. "But he says there's a school of minnows ahead. We can ask them."

They found the minnows in the shallows near a sandy berm. Fawn flew down so that she was just above the water. She tapped on the surface with her toes. When several silvery fish swam up, she leaned down and whispered to them.

Fawn looked up. Her face was triumphant. "They've seen him!"

Lainey's heart leaped. "Are you sure?"

"I asked if a stranger had been through here," Fawn told her. "They described him exactly. Orange with a gold belly. 'Fancy-looking,' they said."

"That's Sunny!" Lainey exclaimed. "Did they say where he went?"

Fawn whispered to the fish again. "They say he was headed for the Wough."

"The wha?" asked Kate, confused.

"The Wough River," Rani explained. "Havendish Stream flows into it. It's not far. But—" She frowned.

"What?" Lainey asked.

"Well, it's a very big river," Rani said. "A little fish like Sunny might get lost there."

Lainey tightened her grip on the fishbowl. "Poor Sunny. Let's hurry!"

Fawn thanked the minnows and they continued downstream. Rani navigated, giving directions like "Paddle to the left. There's a rock underwater" or "It's too shallow

ahead. Keep right so we don't scrape the bottom."

But they scraped anyway. More than once, the girls had to climb out of the raft and carry it through a shallow stretch. Lainey started to worry that they would never make it to the Wough River.

"There's got to be a faster way," Kate said, when they'd climbed back into the boat a third time.

"Fairy dust would make the raft lighter," Fawn pointed out.

"Oh yeah! Why didn't I think of that?" Kate said. "Who has the fairy dust?"

Kate looked at Mia. Mia looked at Lainey. Lainey looked at Gabby.

"Wait a second," Fawn said. "Don't tell me no one brought fairy dust."

"We were so busy with the boat, we forgot," Mia said.

"And I was worried about Sunny," Lainey said.

"*I* brought the food," Gabby reminded them.

"But we're miles away from Pixie Hollow!" Fawn cried. "How will you get back upstream?"

No one had thought of that. "Haven't *you* got any fairy dust?" Mia asked the fairies hesitantly.

But Fawn and Rani had only the dust on their backs. It wasn't enough for all of them.

"Never mind," Rani said firmly. "We'll figure out how to get back later. Look, we've reached the Wough."

Finally! Lainey turned with excitement. Then her heart sank. Ahead was a deep brown river as wide as a city street. How would they ever find Sunny in there?

"There are *two* rivers," Gabby said. Sure enough, just past the point where Havendish Stream joined it, the Wough River split in two.

"Uh-oh," Mia said. "How do we know which way he went?"

Everyone looked at Fawn. But the animal fairy shook her head. "I'm not sure."

"Rani?" Lainey asked.

Rani's pale blue eyes studied the river. "I don't know, either," she said at last.

"Then it's up to you, Lainey," Kate said.

Lainey looked back and forth between

the two branches. She could feel everyone watching her.

Which way had Sunny gone? Which way should *they* go?

Chapter 5

Rani felt troubled. As she stared at the two branches of the river, she had the uneasy feeling she was forgetting something.

"I don't know," Lainey said. She was looking back and forth, too. "What if I pick the wrong way?"

"We'll have to take that chance. Just guess," Fawn said. The current was sweeping them toward the fork in the river.

If they didn't choose a path quickly, the river would choose it for them.

Lainey took a deep breath and pushed up her glasses. "Okay, um . . . right," she said in a quavering voice. "No, left. Left!"

As Kate and Mia paddled to the left, a nervous prickle crept up Rani's spine. She felt as if she was forgetting something important.

The river widened, then slowed to a crawl. They were passing through dense jungle now. Unlike the gentle forest around Pixie Hollow, the trees here were huge and close together. The air was hot. Rani longed to dive into the cool water.

"I could really go for a swim," Kate said, echoing her thoughts.

"Me too." Mia wiped her brow. She

peered at the brown water. "Do you think it's safe?"

"We could ask *him*," Gabby said. She pointed to a tree branch jutting over the river. A large green iguana lay on it, basking in the sun. When Mia saw it, she shrieked.

"What's wrong?" Fawn asked.

"I'm not very fond of lizards," Mia said with a shudder.

As if he knew they were talking about him, the iguana raised his head. Suddenly, he slid off his branch and dropped into the water right next to the boat. Rani watched the tip of his scaly tail disappear below the surface.

"Well," Fawn said, "I guess we know it's safe to swim!"

Everyone stared at the bubbles where the iguana had disappeared. "That's okay," Kate said. "I think I've changed my mind."

Before long, the river widened until the banks were no longer in sight. The water was sluggish and clogged with lily pads. Here and there, dead trees jutted up like the masts of wrecked ships. Giant cypress trees, festooned with moss, cast shadows across their path.

"Where *are* we?" Lainey asked.

"It looks like a swamp," Kate said.

"It *is* a swamp," Rani replied. She had suddenly remembered what was bothering her. One branch of the Wough River led to a dismal place called the Sunken Forest. *And we've just found it,* she thought.

A loud *burrrrrup!* made them all jump.

"What was that?" Mia whispered.

Two more croaks echoed through the swamp. "Frogs!" said Fawn. "Let's find them. Maybe they've seen Sunny!"

Soon they came to another patch of lily pads. Four fat bullfrogs sat on top of them, silently watching the raft approach.

"Are you sure about this, Fawn?" Rani asked. She didn't think the bullfrogs looked very friendly.

"Don't worry. I talk to frogs all the time," Fawn said.

They all watched as Fawn flew up to one of the frogs. She bugged her eyes, puffed out her cheeks, and croaked. *Burrrrup!*

But the frog didn't reply. He sat still as a rock, gazing at Fawn with heavy-lidded eyes.

Fawn tried again. *Burrrup! Burrrup!*

Still the frog said nothing.

Fawn frowned. She turned and spoke to another frog, then a third one. They didn't even blink.

"I don't understand," Fawn said, turning to her friends. "They won't talk to me. I— *Ahh!*"

While her back was turned, the first frog's tongue lashed out. Rani watched in horror as the frog leaped up and grabbed Fawn in his huge mouth.

"Fawn!" everyone screamed.

Fawn was hanging halfway out of the frog's mouth. She looked outraged.

"Let me go, you bully!" she shouted, banging on his lip with her hands.

Burrrup! Burrrup! Burrrup! the other frogs croaked. Rani thought they sounded as if they were laughing.

Finally, the frog opened his mouth. Fawn fluttered to a safe distance, then shook her fist at him. "What's the matter with you?" she shouted.

The frog gazed at her dully.

Fawn flew back to the boat. "Downriver frogs haven't got any manners," she said in disgust. "The bullfrogs in Pixie Hollow would never act that way!"

"Manners?" Rani said. "Fawn, he tried to *eat* you!"

"No, he didn't," Fawn replied. "If he'd wanted to eat me, he could have. He just wanted to give me a scare. I guess they don't like strangers around here."

"Meanies!" Gabby hollered at the frogs. "Why don't you pick on someone your own size!"

The frogs blinked. Suddenly, they leaped off their lily pads and disappeared into the water.

"Way to go, Gabby!" Kate said. "You really told them off."

Fawn frowned. "That's not it. I think something else scared them."

They all looked around. The swamp was still and silent. And yet, Rani couldn't shake the feeling that something was watching them.

"Let's get out of here," Mia said. "This place gives me the creeps."

The girls took up their paddles. But they began to paddle in opposite directions. "Not that way, Kate," Mia said. "That's the way we came."

Kate looked confused. "Are you sure? I could have sworn we came the other way."

"What do you think, Rani?" Mia asked.

"I . . . don't know," Rani said. The swamp looked the same in every direction.

"Look!" Lainey cried suddenly. "There, in the water!"

Rani saw nothing but lily pads. "What is it?" she asked.

"It looked like Sunny!"

"Are you sure?" asked Mia.

"No," Lainey admitted. "But it was bright orange. It *could* have been him."

"Let's wait and see if he comes back," Kate said.

They waited for several minutes. Through the cypress trees, Rani could see the sun sinking lower in the sky. They would need to find their way out of the swamp soon. Rani glanced at Fawn and knew she was thinking the same thing.

"Whatever it was, I don't think it's coming back," Kate said finally.

"Just a little longer," Lainey pleaded.

"It'll be dark soon," Fawn said. "We can't wait."

"But what if it *was* Sunny?" Lainey said. "Maybe he needs our help."

Rani looked back at the murky water. She knew what she had to do.

"I'll go underwater," she said. "I'll look for Sunny myself."

Chapter 6

Rani stood at the edge of the raft, about to dive in.

"Rani, *don't!*" Lainey said. "Those frogs could still be down there."

"And who *knows* what else," Mia added with a shudder.

Rani had thought of that. But she didn't know what else to do. It was her fault Sunny was gone. She owed it to Lainey to look for him. "I'm the only one who can go," she said. "Fawn can't swim. And you girls are all too big. You'd scare all the fish away."

"But we won't be able to see you under the lily pads," Fawn pointed out. "How will we know if you're in trouble?"

Rani thought for a minute. "We'll tie a rope around my waist. If I need help, I'll give it a tug."

For a moment it seemed that the plan wouldn't work when they realized that they didn't have a rope. But then Kate had the idea of using the drawstring from her sweatshirt. She slid it off and double-knotted it around Rani's waist.

"If you feel a tug, even a little one, pull me up *fast*. Got it?" Rani said to Kate.

"I've got it. But I still don't like it," Kate said as she wrapped the other end of the string around her hand. "It feels too much like fishing."

And I'm the bait, Rani thought, but she pushed the thought from her mind. "Ready?"

"Ready." Kate began to lower her toward the water. Rani took a deep breath and—

Splash! Rani opened her eyes. She was in an underwater forest. The long stems of the lily pads rose around her like the trunks of tall, narrow trees.

Something brushed against her foot. Rani whirled around. But it was only her hair, waving behind her.

Stay calm, Rani told herself with a little laugh. *You'll be done in no time.*

Rani swam through the lily pads. She was surprised how peaceful it was in

the swamp. Sunlight filtered down, illuminating the greenish water. A school of tadpoles swam past, their little tails wiggling hard.

What was that? From somewhere came a soft, rhythmic sound, almost like a pulse. Rani tried to listen. But it was hard to hear over the loud beating of her heart.

Ahead in the weeds, something moved. Rani saw a flash of orange. Was it Sunny?

The orange fish came toward her. As it slowly became visible through the murk, Rani's heart seemed to stop. The fish was big enough to swallow her whole!

Rani reached for the rope. But before she could pull it, the fish turned and darted away.

What had scared it?

There was that pulse again. The sound wasn't muffled anymore. Now it sounded crisp and mechanical—and it was getting closer.

TICK-TOCK.

TICK-TOCK.

TICK-TOCK.

Suddenly, Rani knew what it was!

She tugged frantically at the rope.

Even as Kate hauled her out of the water, Rani kept pulling. She gasped as her lungs filled with air.

"Go!" Rani spluttered. "Got . . . to . . . *go!*"

Her friends clustered around her, their faces filled with concern. "Rani?" Fawn said. "What's wrong?"

At last Rani caught her breath. "Crocodile!" she hollered, just as the huge beast surfaced.

The girls screamed. The monster's jaws were open and they could clearly hear the *tick-tock* of the clock he'd swallowed many years ago. Every creature in Never Land knew the croc by that sound.

"Make him go away, Fawn!" Gabby screamed.

"This is no time for talking. He's hunting!" Fawn cried. "Go! Go!"

The girls paddled with all their might. But the crocodile was fast, closing the gap between them. Rani watched as he got closer. He was only three feet away . . . two feet . . . one foot . . .

As the crocodile bumped against the raft, Mia suddenly twisted around. She raised her paddle into the air and brought it down sharply on the croc's snout.

"Get away! Get away, you horrible thing!" she yelled, whacking it again.

The crocodile's mouth closed. He gave the girls a hurt look. *Fine, I won't eat you,* he seemed to be saying. *But you don't have to be so mean about it.* Then he swam away.

Everyone looked at Mia. "Holy guacamole," Kate said. "How did you know that would work?"

"I didn't," Mia admitted.

"Well, then why did you hit him?"

Mia sniffed. "I told you," she said. "I don't like lizards."

Chapter 7

They wasted no time getting out of the swamp. A helpful heron provided directions, but he hadn't seen Sunny. By the time they were back on the Wough River, the sun was behind the trees. With a sinking heart, Lainey realized it would be dark soon.

"We'll have to stop for the night," Rani said. "Even I can't navigate a river in the dark. We can start out again first thing in the morning."

They looked for a place to camp. But the trees grew thick along the river, and they couldn't find a spot to pull over. The first few stars had bobbed up in the evening sky by the time they finally dragged the raft onto a sandy beach.

"Will the crocodile follow us?" Mia asked.

"I doubt it," Fawn said. "He's too lazy. There are plenty of fish for him to eat in the swamp—"

Lainey gulped. "Fish?"

"I don't mean *Sunny*," Fawn said quickly. "He's too small for a crocodile to bother with."

"Speaking of eating, I'm hungry," Kate

said, changing the subject. "Gabby, where's that backpack?"

"Here." Gabby handed over the bag she'd brought from home.

Kate eagerly unzipped it. Then her face fell. "Where's all the food?"

Mia looked over Kate's shoulder. She pulled a package of cookies out of the bag. "Gabby! This is all you brought? You were supposed to pack sandwiches!"

"They're sandwich *cookies*," Gabby pointed out.

Kate looked at the package and sighed. "I could eat, like, ten million cookies right now."

Gabby frowned. "Then *you* should have packed the food."

"It's okay, Gabby," Lainey said, even though her stomach was growling, too. "I *like* having cookies for dinner."

They sat down to their meager meal. Rani and Fawn had one cookie each. Mia divided the rest evenly between the girls.

"Wait," said Kate. "What about those?" She pointed to six cookies Mia had left in the package.

"Those," said Mia, "are for breakfast."

"But I'm hungry now," Kate complained.

"You'll be even hungrier tomorrow," Mia pointed out.

The others sighed, but they knew Mia was right. They gobbled up their cookies, then sat picking at the crumbs.

"I wish we had a fire," Gabby said. "When we go camping with Mami and Papi, we always have a fire."

"I heard you can make one by rubbing two sticks together," said Kate.

She found two sticks, and the girls all took turns trying to start a fire. But they couldn't make so much as a single spark. Fawn tried, too, using two tiny twigs, but she couldn't start one, either. Rani didn't even try.

"I'm a water fairy," she said. "We're not good with fire."

There was nothing to do then but try to sleep. Rani and Fawn curled up inside some nearby flowers. The girls stretched out on the sand and watched the rest of the stars emerge. Luckily, it was a warm night. Fawn hummed a special song to keep the mosquitoes away. All in all, Lainey knew it could be worse.

Still, as the night grew darker, so did Lainey's thoughts. There had been no news about Sunny since they'd reached the Wough River. And they'd lost hours in the swamp. *Maybe this whole trip is pointless,* Lainey thought. What chance did they really have of finding him?

Lainey searched out the brightest star in the sky and made a wish. *Please let Sunny be okay. Please let him be safe until I can find him.*

Lainey knew her wish might not come

true. She knew little fish were eaten by big fish, and those fish were eaten by even bigger ones—it was the way of the wild. But she couldn't help wishing anyway.

After a time, Lainey noticed a patch of sky that was darker than the rest. Something was blotting out the stars.

"Kate," she whispered. "Are you asleep?"

"No."

"What is that?" She pointed to the patch of darkness. It seemed to be moving.

Kate was quiet. "I dunno," she said at last.

"A cloud, maybe?" Mia was watching it, too.

"It looks like it has arms,"  Gabby said. "And legs."

The girls gasped as the dark shape suddenly

swooped toward them. A second later a boy dressed all in leaves landed on the sand.

"Peter!" the girls cried, leaping up.

It was Peter Pan, of course, the boy who lived on Never Land and never grew old. The last time Lainey and her friends had seen him, he'd been headed out to sea on a ghost ship.

"Did you make it all the way around the world?" Kate asked him.

"What?" Peter blinked.

"On the ghost ship. Did you sail it around the world?"

"Oh no," Peter said. "I hardly made it past the Viridian Sea when I was set upon by pirates. It was an epic battle!" He leaped around, slashing his arm through the air like a sword to show just how epic it was. "You should have seen it."

"The *Viridian* Sea?" Mia whispered to Lainey. "We learned all the oceans in school. I've never heard of that one."

Lainey shrugged. She knew what Mia meant. You could never be sure if Peter had all his facts straight. But it didn't matter much. He was a great storyteller.

"Where's the ship now?" Lainey asked.

"Gone," Peter said. "Sunk by cannon fire."

"Oh no!" Kate gasped. "Not that awesome ship!"

Peter just grinned. "Yes. It was fantastic watching it go down."

When Gabby asked if Peter knew how to make a fire, he said, "Do I!" and set to

work at once. He expertly spun the sticks and flames leaped up, as if by magic. The girls roused Fawn and Rani from their flowers. They were glad to see Peter, too—he often visited Pixie Hollow to get fairy dust for flying.

They all added sticks until the campfire was a crackling blaze. As they sat around it, Peter entertained them with stories about his adventures with the Lost Boys. Soon, the fire had dried the girls' clothes, and the laughter had lifted their damp spirits.

Lainey and her friends told Peter why they were on the river. "You'll let us know if you see my Sunny, won't you?" Lainey said. "He's bright orange with a gold belly."

"I saw a fish like that just this afternoon," Peter said.

"Really?" Lainey squinted at him. Was he telling the truth, or was this just another tale? "Where?"

"Oh, that way." Peter waved an arm downstream. "He seemed happy. Eating everything in sight."

"That *does* sound like Sunny!" For the first time since they'd left the swamp, Lainey felt hopeful.

They talked a while longer, but by then it was very late. Lainey's eyelids grew heavier and heavier, until at last she couldn't hold them open anymore.

∗

Lainey woke with the first light. Kate, Gabby, and Mia were still asleep in the sand, lying in a circle around the campfire. The fairies were curled in their petal beds. Peter was gone. *Off on some new adventure, probably,* Lainey thought.

Lainey woke her friends. Then she went down to the river's edge. She splashed cold water on her face, then stood for a moment, watching the river. *Sunny's somewhere just ahead,* she told herself. *We're going to find him today.*

As she was making her way back up the sand, she suddenly hear Mia exclaim, "Oh no! The cookies are gone!"

"What?" Everyone rushed to her. They looked with dismay at the empty

"Peter must have taken them," Mia said glumly.

"That rat!" Kate scowled. "I never thought he was a thief."

"He's not." Mia pointed to the ground nearby, where a small pile of coconuts sat.

"Breakfast!" Gabby exclaimed, grabbing one.

"Look," Lainey said. "He left something else, too."

She picked up a small bundle wrapped in leaves and tied with a piece of grass. Lainey carefully undid the bow. The leaves were full of fairy dust.

Chapter 8

Their hearts were light as they set off again. Sitting in her cup holder, Rani thought the raft seemed lighter, too. No doubt it was because they'd all sprinkled themselves with fairy dust. Fairy dust made everything lighter.

It was another bright, cloudless day. There was no shade on the river. As the sun climbed higher, Rani grew uncomfortably warm. She swept her long hair up and tied it atop her head so she could fan her neck.

After a while, she became aware that Gabby was staring at her. "Do they hurt?" Gabby asked.

"What? Oh." Rani realized that Gabby was looking at the stumps of her wings. "No, they don't hurt."

"Then why can't you fly?" Gabby asked.

"Gabby! Don't be rude," Mia scolded.

"I'm not being rude," Gabby told her. "I was just wondering. None of us have wings—well, except for me, and mine are just pretend. But we can all fly if we have fairy dust. So why can't Rani?"

"It's okay," Rani said to Mia, who was gaping at her sister in embarrassment. "I don't mind telling you. I've tried flying. But it's not the same as flying with wings."

Rani remembered how dizzy and off-balance she'd felt the few times she'd tried to fly, as if she'd plummet to the ground at any moment.

"Anyway, I'm used to not having them now," Rani went on. "When I need to fly somewhere, I call my bird friend, Brother Dove. He carries me."

"But you must miss flying! I bet we could teach you," Kate said.

Rainey sighed. She knew Kate meant well. But it was still frustrating. Others were always trying to find a way to fix her, just because she was different. They thought she'd be better off if she were more like them. But Rani liked the way she was. She liked being able to swim, and she liked flying with Brother Dove. Sometimes she even felt lucky for not having wings. She was able to do things no other fairy could do.

"That's okay, Kate," Rani replied. "But I like the way I am."

The raft dipped as they went over a small ledge. The current had picked up. The water turned white as it rushed over and around the rocks.

"Everybody hang on," Kate said.

"Wheeeee!" cried Gabby.

"Wait a minute," Rani said, frowning. Her pointed ears pricked up, tuning in to a louder roar. "I don't like the sound of that. . . ."

They came around a bend. Ahead, large rocks jutted up from the river. The water roiled around them. It shot through the narrow gaps between the rocks in a gush of foaming white.

"We can't go through those rapids! We'll be smashed to pieces!" Fawn said.

Kate and Mia dug in their paddles. They steered the little raft over to the bank. When they were all safe, Kate and Fawn got out and scouted ahead.

"We'll have to go around this part," Kate reported when they came back. "There are too many rocks."

They took to the air. Lainey carried Rani, while Kate and Mia dragged the raft. Though it wasn't heavy, it was awkward to carry. They kept bumping into each other.

"Why don't you just put some fairy dust on it so it floats?" Gabby suggested.

"Of course!" Kate said. "Good idea, Gabby. Why didn't I think of that?"

They sprinkled fairy dust on the raft and it bobbed into the air. Kate tied the string from her sweatshirt to it and pulled it along like a balloon. After that, they moved it easily past the rocks.

On the other side, the river flattened out again. It was clear enough that Rani could see all the way to the bottom.

"Do you think this is where Peter saw Sunny?" Lainey asked as they all got back into the raft.

"It could be," Fawn said. "Let's keep an eye out for him."

Rani peered over the side of the boat. She saw eyes, a nose, and a mouth reflected in the water. Rani smiled. Her reflection smiled back at her—then darted away. Rani gasped. "What?"

"Look!" Lainey pointed. Tiny creatures were playing on the surface of the river. They had arms and legs like fairies, but they looked as if they were made of water.

"Water sprites," Fawn said. She looked worried.

But the girls didn't notice her frown. "They're so cute!" exclaimed Mia.

"Listen to them talking," Kate said. The sprites were calling to each other in plinks, plops, and splashes.

"Let's keep going," Fawn said.

Rani knew why Fawn was concerned. Water sprites were tricksters. Once, a water sprite had even fooled Rani into looking after a whole flock of clouds. The clouds had rained on Pixie Hollow for days, and all the fairies had been upset.

But these water sprites didn't seem to be doing any harm, Rani thought. They looked as if they were just out having fun. Some danced across the surface of the water. Others ran ahead, as if trying to outrace the raft.

"We should ask them if they've seen Sunny," Lainey said.

Fawn shook her head. "They won't help us. Water sprites never help fairies."

"Really?" Kate said. "Why?"

"They're jealous because we have wings," Fawn explained.

"Well, I don't have wings," Rani said. "So maybe they'll talk to me. Yoo-hoo! Hello!" She waved at the sprites. "Can you help us? We're looking for someone."

But the sprites carried on dancing and playing.

"See?" said Fawn. "I told you."

"Maybe they just don't understand," Rani said. "I have an idea."

She collected a few drops of water from the side of the raft and rolled them together into a ball. Then she began to pinch and pull the water, shaping it with her hands. Three fins appeared, then a long fluid tail.

"It's a fish!" Gabby said.

Rani flecked a pinch of fairy dust over the water fish. It shimmered orange and gold.

"It looks just like Sunny!" Lainey exclaimed.

"We'll show this to the water sprites.

Maybe they'll tell us where he is," Rani said.

But when the sprites saw the watery model of Sunny, they only smiled. One of them picked up a few drops of water and juggled them in the air.

"They think we're just playing," Lainey said.

"Let me try," said Kate. "HAVE. YOU.

SEEN. THIS. FISH?" she yelled to the water sprites. She pointed at the river and then pantomimed a fish swimming with her hands.

The sprites laughed again. They raced and tumbled along beside the raft, never once losing contact with the water.

"It's no use," Rani said. She dropped the model of Sunny into the water. It swam away from the boat for a few feet, then dissolved.

Rani had been dimly aware of a far-off rushing sound, a little like wind blowing through the trees. But she'd been too distracted by the sprites to give it much thought. Only when the rush became a roar did she pay attention.

"Oh no," she said.

Now the others heard the sound, too.

"What's that?" asked Kate. "It sounds like more rapids!"

But it wasn't rapids. Ahead, the river dropped away into nothing.

"WATERFALL!" Fawn yelled.

The water sprites were gone. The current was fast now, speeding them toward the edge. There was no time to pull off the river. No time to do anything but—

"Fly!" Kate hollered, dropping her paddle. "Now!"

I can't *fly!* Rani thought. But a second later, Lainey's hands closed around her. Holding Rani, Lainey leaped from the raft, along with Fawn and the other girls.

They hovered above the river. Rani was so relieved to be safe that for a moment she didn't understand why everyone was shouting.

Gabby was still in the raft. She sat, frozen stiff, as she hurtled toward the waterfall. Her eyes were wide with terror.

"Fly, Gabby!" the other girls screamed. "Fly! Fly!"

But it was too late. The raft plunged over the edge, with Gabby still inside.

Chapter 9

"Oh my gosh," Lainey whispered. Her heart plummeted as she watched Gabby drop out of sight.

Kate had gone pale. Mia's expression was too awful to look at.

Together, the three friends raced to the waterfall. Holding hands, they peered over the edge.

"OH MY GOSH!" Lainey shouted.

The raft was floating, just a few feet

down from the waterfall's edge. Gabby was still sitting inside, getting soaked by spray. When she heard their voices, she turned and looked up at them.

"I'm okay," she said. "But I don't know how to get down."

Mia flew over and hugged her sister. "I don't understand how this happened."

"It's the fairy dust." Rani spoke up from Lainey's hands. "It made the raft lighter than air. When you all jumped out, it floated. It was only your weight that was holding it down."

"Gabby isn't heavy enough to weigh it down on her own," Fawn added. "Lucky for us."

"Come on, Gabby. Let's get you out of there," Kate said. "Do you think you can fly if I hold your hand?"

"Wait!" said Lainey. "If Gabby gets out now, the raft might float away. And we still need it to find Sunny."

Kate thought for a moment. "I have an idea." She climbed into the raft next to Gabby. The raft slowly began to sink.

"Come on!" she called to her friends. "One at a time."

Mia climbed in next. The raft sank faster. When Lainey climbed in, holding Rani, the raft splashed onto the water below. Fawn fluttered down and joined them.

They'd landed in a calm, beautiful lagoon. Large rocks jutted up from the middle. Lainey noticed creatures lying on top of the rocks, sunning themselves. "Are those—?"

"Mermaids." Rani nodded.

"They're *beautiful*!" Mia gushed.

They are *pretty,* Lainey thought. The mermaids had long, shiny blue-green hair. The scales of their shimmering tails were all different colors—violet, turquoise, silver, green. One mermaid's tail was even reddish-gold.

"I can't believe we're finally going to

meet a mermaid," Mia said, amazed. Lainey knew her friend had always wanted to meet one.

Fawn snorted. "I wouldn't count on that."

"What do you mean?" Mia asked.

"Mermaids are snobs," Fawn said. "They won't even talk to fairies. And they like Clumsies even less."

"They're not *all* snobs, Fawn," Rani said. "I think we should talk to them. Maybe one of them can help us."

"I guess it's worth a try," said Fawn.

But as they paddled toward them, the mermaids slid into the water, one by one.

"Wait!" Mia called after them. "We just want to talk to you."

"We're looking for someone!" Kate added.

The mermaids ignored them. Every time the raft got close, they dove into the water. Their long tails were the last things to disappear.

Finally, only one mermaid remained, sitting on the farthest rock. She had greenish gold scales. A pink starfish was fixed in her hair like a bow. She watched with a bored expression as Lainey and her friends paddled toward her.

When they got close to her rock, the mermaid started to dive.

"Wait!" Lainey cried. "Please wait! I'm just trying to find my pet goldfish."

The mermaid hesitated.

"He's bright orange with a gold belly," Lainey continued, before the mermaid could leave. "And his top fin sticks straight up. His name is Sunny, and I'm really worried about him. Have you seen him?"

The mermaid looked at her with an expression Lainey couldn't read. Then, suddenly, she opened her mouth and called something in a strange language. To Lainey, it sounded like *Oooooaaooooooooooooooaaaanaaanaaa.*

Across the lagoon, the water stirred. Something big was moving through it. Lainey clutched the side of the raft. Whatever was coming, she wasn't sure she wanted to see it.

The mermaid called again. *Ooooooaaoooooooooooooaaaanaaanaaa.*

The raft rocked as a huge fish surfaced

next to them. The fish was almost as big as Lainey. It had orange scales and a gold belly. Its top fin stuck up in a funny way.

Lainey would have known that fin anywhere. "It's Sunny!"

Chapter 10

"*That's* Sunny?" Gabby asked in astonishment.

"It can't be," Kate said. "Sunny is little. This fish is a monster!"

Lainey was just as confused as her friends. She was sure this was her pet. But how had he gotten so big?

"You shouldn't let your goldfish loooose," the mermaid said. She had a strange accent, but Lainey could understand her. "They eat tooooo much. When I fooound him, he was gobbling everything in the lagooooon. It's not fair to the other fish."

"I'm sorry," Lainey said. "I didn't mean to let him go. He just got away from me."

"Sunny got this big just by *eating*?" Mia turned to Fawn. "Is that even possible?"

"I suppose so," Fawn said. "After all, he's been eating his way down the river. And Never Land's magic may have helped, too."

Sunny was swimming briskly around the raft. "I think he's glad to see you again," Fawn told Lainey.

"He is?" Lainey felt a rush of happiness. "Did he say that?"

"Not exactly," Fawn said. "Goldfish

don't talk. But I can see how excited he is. Goldfish have excellent hearing, you know. He probably recognizes your voice from his time in the fishbowl."

"Oh no." Lainey's happy feeling evaporated. She'd been so glad to see that Sunny was all right, she'd forgotten one thing. "He'll *never* fit into his fishbowl now."

"He'd need a bowl the size of your house," Kate agreed.

"I can't take him home," Lainey said. "What will my parents say?"

"Lainey, I have an idea," Rani said. She beckoned her closer. When Lainey leaned down, the water fairy whispered in her ear.

Lainey nodded. Though it made her sad, she knew it was the right thing to do. She turned to the mermaid and asked, "Will you take care of my goldfish? He could be your pet, if you want."

The mermaid looked at her for a moment, then nodded. It was hard to tell from her expression, but Lainey thought she seemed pleased.

Lainey leaned over the side of the raft. She reached down and ran her fingers through the water. "I'm sorry I can't take you with me, Sunny," she said. "But I think you'll be okay here. I promise I'll come and visit."

The mermaid slid off her rock. She said something to Sunny in her strange language. Then, together, they started to swim away.

Lainey watched them leave, feeling an

ache in her chest. She wished there had been a better way to say good-bye.

"Wait!" she yelled. "Wait!"

The mermaid stopped swimming and looked back at her. Sunny stopped, too.

Lainey took off the life jacket. She took off her shoes and handed her glasses to Mia. Then she jumped into the lagoon. She splashed through the water toward Sunny. Lainey wasn't a great swimmer. Compared to the mermaid, Lainey knew she looked silly and graceless. But she didn't care.

Sunny raced back toward her. Lainey treaded water as he swam a circle around her. She laughed when he bumped her with his nose. "Hey! That tickles!"

They swam and splashed and chased each other through the water. When

Lainey finally grew tired, she swam back to the raft. Her friends helped pull her inside.

"Good-bye, Sunny," Lainey told him. "Be a good fish, okay?"

They watched together as Sunny and the mermaid swam out of sight.

"I guess we can fly back to Pixie Hollow from here," Fawn said finally. "Are you all ready?"

"Ready," the girls said in unison.

They rose into the air. Lainey carried Rani. Mia held Gabby's hand. And Kate pulled the floating raft behind her.

As they crossed the Mermaid Lagoon, Lainey looked down one last time. Deep in the water, she could see the great coral castle where the mermaids lived.

From this height, the lagoon looked a little like Sunny's old goldfish bowl.

Sunny was going to be happy in his new home. Lainey was sure of it.

✳

"Start from the beginning, Lainey," Kate said. "Tell us what your parents said."

It was a few days after their river adventure. Lainey and her friends were sitting on the floor in Lainey's bedroom.

"At first they didn't understand when I said Sunny was gone," Lainey explained. "My mom kept asking, 'What do you mean? Where did he go?'"

"You didn't tell her about Never Land, did you?" Mia asked.

Lainey shook her head. "I just said that

Sunny was in a happier place now."

Kate laughed. "Well, it's true. Though it sounds a little different when you put it that way."

"My parents thought so, too," Lainey said. "They gave me big hugs and asked if I was all right. Mom said goldfish sometimes had short lives. She said maybe we should have started with a different pet. So that's how I ended up with this little guy."

Lainey held up her new hamster. He had white fur with brown patches. His bright eyes looked like two little black beads. "I just had to promise that I'll be extra careful not to let him get loose in the house," she explained.

"Or anywhere else—like Never Land," Kate added.

"What are you going to name him?" Gabby asked.

"How about Zippy?" Kate suggested.

"Or Patches?" said Mia.

"Name him Spike!" said Gabby. "Spike is a good name for a hamster."

"Those are all good names," Lainey said. "But I was thinking of calling him Lucky. Because I'm lucky to have him." She held up her hamster so they were almost nose to nose. "From now on, your name is Lucky Spike Zippy Patches Hamster."

Lucky wiggled his whiskers. "I think he likes it," Mia said.

"Hello, Lucky," Gabby said, gently stroking his head.

They all took turns petting Lucky one more time. Then Lainey placed him back in his cage, checking to make sure the door was latched tight.

"Come on," she said, standing up.

"Where are we going?" asked Kate.

"To Never Land, of course," Lainey replied with a grin. "I can't wait to tell the fairies all about my new pet!"

Read this Sneak peek of IN the Game, the next Never Girls adventure!

Kate was having her best soccer practice ever. She was the first one to finish the warm-up laps. Then she juggled the ball thirty-three times with her feet without dropping it.

Kate hoped Coach Christy noticed. It was the last practice before the first game of the season, and today the coach was going to assign their positions. Kate wanted to play goalkeeper. She loved being the protector of the net—in the most critical moments of a soccer game, it was all up to the keeper. The few seconds when she was the only thing between an opponent and the goal were the most exciting parts of the game.

But there were at least two other girls who wanted to be goalie. Kate knew the coach might choose one of them. That was why she had to be at the top of her game.

She waited nervously as the coach passed out pinnies and divided the team up for a scrimmage. "Kate, you'll play keeper today," Coach Christy said, handing her a red mesh shirt.

"Yesss!" Kate pumped her fist and ran

to stand in front of the two orange cones that marked the goal. She was going to show the coach what she could really do!

The two sides kicked off. For a while, Kate watched the action eagerly. But as the game wore on, she began to grow impatient. Her teammates were playing great defense. In fact, they'd been so good at keeping the ball away from the goal, Kate had nothing to do! How was Coach going to know to put her in as goalkeeper for the real game if she couldn't see her shine?

"C'mon," Kate whispered, willing the ball to come her way. She braced as the yellow team's striker drove toward the goal. But the red team's sweeper moved in and blocked the shot.

Kate sighed and put her hands on her hips as the ball traveled back down the field. Her mind wandered to Pixie Hollow. *Too bad Coach couldn't see me do that bicycle kick,* she thought. She smiled, imagining the looks on her teammates' faces if she pulled off something like that.

"Kate! Heads up!" Coach Christy shouted.

Kate snapped to attention. The ball was flying toward her and— Oh no! While she'd been daydreaming, she'd moved all the way to the front of the penalty box. She'd left the goal wide open!

Kate leaped into the air, but she knew it was too late. The ball was high over her head. There was no way she could—

Thwump! The ball landed squarely in Kate's arms.

Kate's feet hit the ground and there was a second of stunned silence. Her teammates stared at her. Kate was just as surprised as they were. *How did I do that?* she wondered.

"Go, Kate!"

"Holy cow!"

"You really flew!"

Flew? Kate thought with a jolt. *Oh no. The fairy dust!* Usually in Never Land she flew until she dropped from the sky and there wasn't a speck of magical dust left on her. But they'd left in such a hurry because of Gabby's bloody nose, Kate had forgotten she still had dust on her—until now. She really *had* flown to catch the ball!

Coach clapped her hands. "Okay, Fireballs," she hollered. "Bring it in."

As Kate jogged over with the rest of the team, she kept her eyes on the ground. She was afraid to look at her teammates.

Could they tell? she wondered. Did they know she had magic? What would happen if the secret of Pixie Hollow got out?

"Nice playing today, everyone," the coach said when the team was gathered around. "Kate . . ."

Kate slowly raised her eyes.

"Incredible save! That's the kind of hustle we need for our game against Westside Thunder on Saturday," Coach Christy said, beaming. "I'm putting you in as goalkeeper."

"I, uh . . . um . . . ," Kate stammered. She knew she should say something about what had happened. But she couldn't find the right words.

The coach seemed to think she was just excited. "It's going to be a tough first game," she told the team. "But I know you've all got what it takes. We're going to have a great season, girls. Now go home and get some rest. See you all on Saturday."

As practice broke up, Kate lingered behind. "Coach Christy," she said, finding her voice. "I'm not sure I can, um . . . make another save like that."

The coach raised her eyebrows. "Why not?"

"Well . . ." Kate tried to think of a reason that would sound good. "I think that was kind of a one-time thing."

The coach zipped up the red windbreaker she always wore. "If you can do it once, you can do it again. In all my years of coaching soccer, I've never seen a save like that. You have a natural talent, Kate."

"I wouldn't exactly say *natural*," Kate mumbled.

"The Thunders are a tough team to beat," Coach Christy went on. "We'll need to use every advantage. But I think with you as keeper, we have a really good chance. What do you say?"

Kate hesitated. The coach was counting on her. How could she say no?

"I guess so," she mumbled.

"Don't look so worried," Coach Christy said. "We're going to have a great game."

Kate tried to smile. But she *was* worried. Coach Christy was expecting another amazing save in the game against the Westside Thunders. Kate was good at soccer, but she wasn't *that* good. Her skills alone wouldn't be enough.

There was only one way she was going to be able to play like she had today. She was going to need more fairy dust.